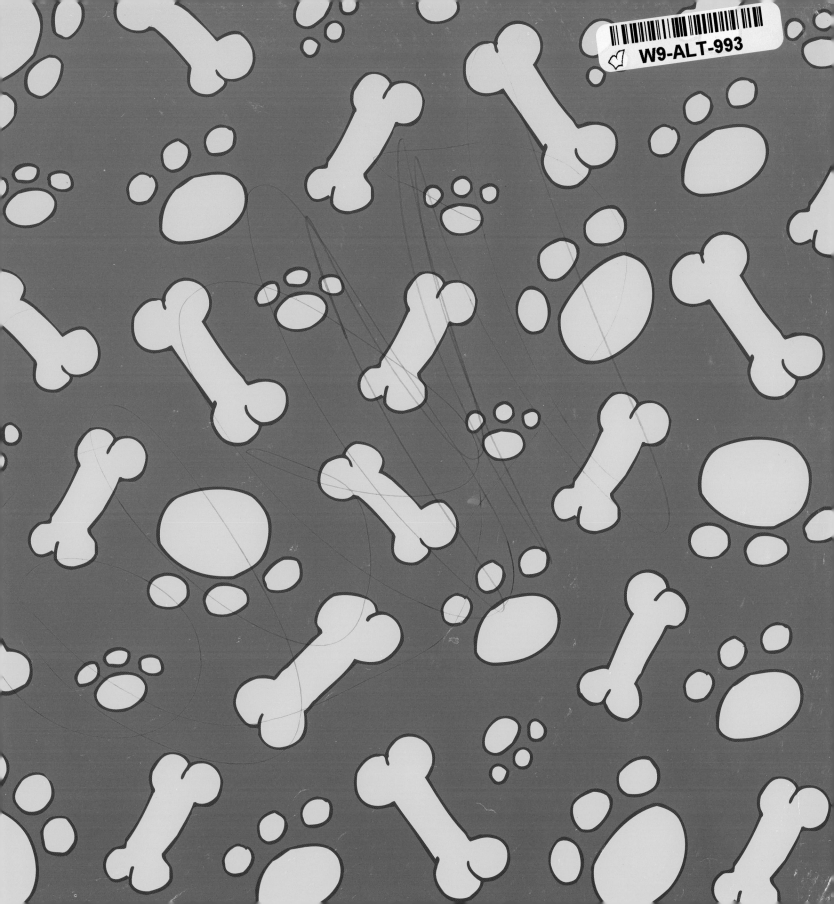

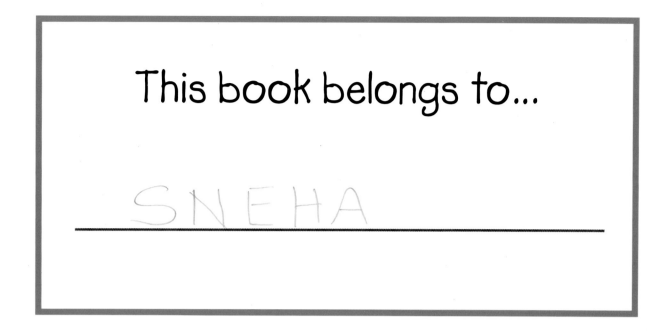

This book belongs to...

SNEHA

ALLEY DOGS

Big Top

Bright ☆ Sparks

This is a Bright Sparks Book
First published in 2000
BRIGHT SPARKS, Queen Street House, 4 Queen Street, Bath BA1 1HE, UK

Copyright © PARRAGON 2000

Created and produced by THE COMPLETE WORKS,
St. Mary's Road, Royal Leamington Spa, Warwickshire CV31 1JP, UK

Editorial Director: Mike Phipps
Project Manager: Stuart Branch
Editor: Aneurin Rhys
Designer: Anne Matthews

ISBN 1-84250-009-0

Big Top

Written by Lesley Rees
Illustrated by Terry Burton

Bright ☆ Sparks

It was a grey day in the tumble-down, messy alley. Harvey and his gang were fed up!

"I'm bored!" groaned Ruffles. "There's nothing to do!"

"What about a game of hide-and-go-seek?" asked Harvey.

"Boring! Boring! Boring!" called Puddles, hanging upside down on the fence.

"What we need is some fun!" Bonnie yawned. "I've got an idea..."

Soon Bonnie and Puddles were jumping on an old mattress. BOINGG! BOINGG! BOINGG! They bounced up and down, up and down.

"*This* is fun!" shrieked Puddles. "I bet I can bounce the highest."

"I'm the *Amazing Bouncing Bonnie*," Bonnie giggled. "Look!"

She bounced high into the air – and landed with a thud on a clump of grass! "Ooops!" she said. "I think I missed!"

Then Mac clambered onto the washing line.

"WHEEEE! Look at me! I'm a wibbly wobbly dog."

"Oh no!" Patchy gasped. "Here comes tumble time," as Mac toppled over onto the mattress below. Mac sat up and rubbed his head, grinning.

Harvey laughed. His friends' tricks had given him an idea. "Let's put on a circus," he said.

The Alley Dogs all agreed and they scampered off to the playground in search of their big top!

"Okay, everyone," said Harvey, when they arrived. "We need to make a circus ring."

"Do you think these old tyres will make good seats?" asked Ruffles.

"They sure will," said Patchy. "And these old plastic bags can be the curtains!"

In no time at all, the big top was ready.

"Good work!" smiled Harvey.

"We must let everyone know the circus is in town!" said Harvey. "Come on, Ruffles, you've got the loudest voice."

So, Ruffles took a deep breath and boomed out loud, "Roll up! Roll up! Come to Harvey's Big Top. See the Greatest Show on Earth!"

Soon the air was filled with woofing and yapping as their pals lined up to see the circus!

The nervous gang huddled behind the curtain.

"Right," said Harvey. "Who's going first?"

Patchy peeped out. "Not me!" she whispered.
"There are too many dogs out there and I'm shy."

"And I'm still practicing!" cried Ruffles.

The others shook their heads. No one wanted to go first. They were all *scaredy cats*!

Harvey took a deep breath and stepped into the ring. "And now, ladies and gentlemen," he cried, "please give a big, warm woof for *Harvey's Amazing Daring Dogs!*"

The audience clapped and stamped their paws! But the gang did not appear.

"Harvey," Mac called, "we've got doggy tummy-wobbles!"

Harvey crept behind the curtain. His friends were quivering and quaking. "Silly things," he smiled. "There's nothing to be scared of. Watch me."

He quickly pulled on a cape and ran back into the ring.

"Let the show begin with *Harvey the Brave*!" he cried, and the audience gave a loud cheer.

"For my first trick," he announced, "the *Tricky Tightrope!*"

He wiggled and wobbled across the top of the swing from one end to the other — and didn't fall off once.

"How does he do it?" gasped the audience, holding their breath in wonder. "Whatever next?"

Harvey climbed to the top of a huge pile of bricks.

"Eeek! What if he falls?" squeaked a little dog. "I can't bear to look."

But Harvey made it — *and* balanced on one paw!

The Alley Dogs peeped out from behind the curtain. Harvey was having such a good time that it didn't look in the least bit scary. So at last, *Harvey's Amazing Daring Dogs* rushed to join in the fun.

"Look at me," said Ruffles. "I can balance a ball on my tummy."

The audience laughed and cheered and clapped.

Patchy and Mac tumbled and turned on their bouncy mattress – what a pair of acrobats!

The show ended with the dangerous and daring *Trolley Trick*. Everyone held their breath. Bonnie and Ruffles stood on the bottom, Patchy and Mac climbed onto their shoulders and little Puddles balanced on the very tip top. When they were ready, Harvey pushed the trolley around and around the ring.

"More! More!" roared the crowd, as the show came to an end.

"Well, Puddles," smiled Harvey, when they finally got back to their tumble-down, messy alley, "was that boring, boring, boring?"

"Oh no, Harvey," she said. "It wasn't boring, it was fun, fun, fun!"

The End

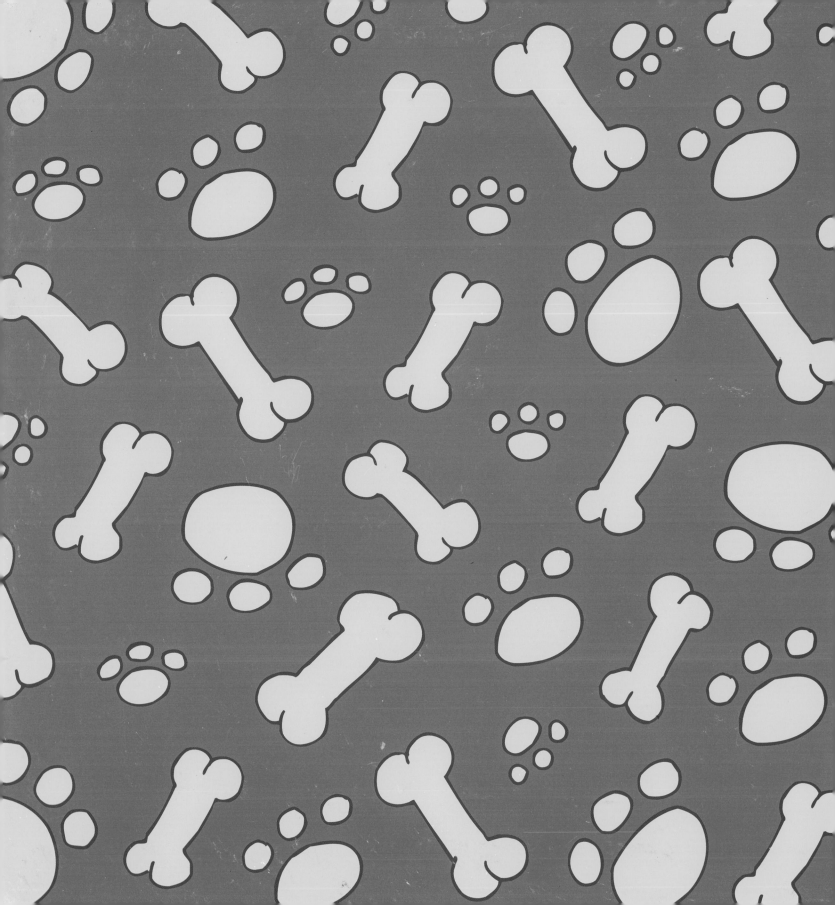